The Big Splash

Written by Maureen Haselhurst
Illustrated by Nick Schon

Collins

She is getting her boat.

She is getting her shark.

She is getting her armbands.

She is getting her flippers.

She is getting her goggles.

She is getting in the bath.

In the bath

boat

shark

flippers

goggles

armbands

15

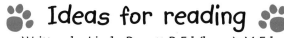 Ideas for reading

Written by Linda Pagett B.Ed (hons), M.Ed
Lecturer and Educational Consultant

Reading objectives:
- read and understand simple sentences
- use phonic knowledge to decode regular words and read them aloud accurately
- demonstrate understanding when talking with others about what they have read

Communication and language objectives:
- express themselves effectively, showing awareness of listeners' needs
- listen to stories, accurately anticipating key events and respond to what they hear with relevant comments, questions or actions
- develop their own narratives and explanations by connecting ideas or events

Curriculum links: Personal, social and emotional development; Knowledge and Understanding of the World

High frequency words: she, is , big, the

Interest words: boat, shark, armbands, flippers, goggles

Word count: 32

Resources: whiteboard, bath items in a bag, e.g. rubber duck and toy boat

Build a context for reading

- Look at the front cover together, discussing what the story might be about.
- Read the title together and discuss what the main character is (a baby dinosaur).
- Walk through the book together, looking at the pictures and naming the objects the baby dinosaur gets out of her bag as she gets ready.
- Write these words on a whiteboard and practise reading them together.
- Ask the children to look quickly through the book, to find the words and pictures. You could use pp14–15 as a support.

Understand and apply reading strategies

- Return to the front cover and read together through the book to p13, modelling one-to-one matching.
- Ask the children to read the story again, independently and quietly, using their finger to point to each word. Listen in and observe, praising expression and prompting decoding strategies if appropriate.